OLIVIA
Makes Memories

Adapted by Lauren Forte
Based on the screenplay "Olivia Explores the Attic" written by Joan Considine-Johnson
Illustrated by Patrick Spaziante

Simon Spotlight
New York   London   Toronto   Sydney   New Delhi

Based on the TV series OLIVIA™
as seen on Nickelodeon™

SIMON SPOTLIGHT
An imprint of Simon & Schuster Children's Publishing Division
1230 Avenue of the Americas, New York, New York 10020
First Simon Spotlight paperback edition October 2015
OLIVIA™ Ian Falconer Ink Unlimited, Inc. and © 2015 Ian Falconer and Classic Media, LLC
All rights reserved, including the right of reproduction in whole or in part in any form.
SIMON SPOTLIGHT and colophon are registered trademarks of Simon & Schuster, Inc.
For information about special discounts for bulk purchases, please contact
Simon & Schuster Special Sales at 1-866-506-1949 or business@simonandschuster.com.
Manufactured in the United States of America 0815 LAK
1 2 3 4 5 6 7 8 9 10
ISBN 978-1-4814-4311-1
ISBN 978-1-4814-4312-8 (eBook)

One afternoon, Olivia and her grandmother were lying on the grass in the yard, looking up at the clouds in the sky.

"Look, Grandma. That one looks like a genie coming out of a bottle," Olivia said. "And over there is an elephant in a tutu."

"You're right, Olivia. That one right there looks like my old steamer trunk," Grandma added.

"Was your trunk like mine?" asked Olivia.

"Yes, it was, but I used it for a time capsule," Grandma replied.

"A time capsule?" asked Olivia. "What's that?"

"Well, people pick things from the time they are living in, and they put them away in a box or a trunk. Years later they open it up to see how much things have changed," explained Grandma. "I made my time capsule when I was just about your age."

"Where is your time capsule now?" Olivia asked.

Grandma shook her head. "I don't know, but I'm sure it's around somewhere."

"Come on, Ian!" said Olivia.
"Let's go find Grandma's
steamer trunk!"
If I were Grandma's time
capsule where would I be?
Olivia wondered.

Olivia and Ian explored everywhere they could think of in the house.
"It's not in William's room," announced Olivia.

"The time capsule is not in the bathroom, either," added Ian.

Olivia and Ian crawled through the living room and took a peek under the couch. "Nice to see you kids playing together," Dad said.

Next, they went into the kitchen and Olivia checked all around.

"Olivia, what are you doing?" Mom asked.

"I'm looking for Grandma's time capsule," Olivia replied.

"I can assure you it's definitely not in the sink," Mom said.

Olivia was frustrated. "Grandma said her time capsule has to be here somewhere, since this house used to be her house."

"We've looked everywhere," Ian said.

"Everywhere except . . . the attic!" Olivia announced.

In the attic, Olivia started opening up all the different boxes and looking inside them. "This isn't it," Olivia said. "It's a bunch of books. And this one has dishes."

Olivia was not giving up though. "I wish I had a map to help me find the time capsule," she said.

Olivia imagined that she and Ian were off exploring a faraway land. They had a map that would lead them to an old and secret buried treasure.

"The map says the treasure is right here," Olivia declared.

She and Ian gazed around in the shadowy stone room. Then they both saw the dusty, old trunk in the corner at the same time.

"Aha! The treasure!" Olivia shouted.

Ian sneezed.

"This is it! We found Grandma's time capsule!" cried Olivia. She and Ian opened the trunk and began to look at the things their grandmother had put inside when she was young girl.

Olivia held up a black round disc.

"What is that?" asked Ian.

"I'm not sure," Olivia answered, "but it could go with this." She put the black disc on a machine, turned it on, and music came out.

"Whoa! Cool!" Ian said as he started dancing.

Olivia found a red-striped Hula-Hoop, and then she saw some clothes near the bottom.

"Is this what Grandma wore?" she asked.

She found an old framed picture of her grandmother wearing the very same clothes!

"I guess so!" Olivia was excited.

"Grandma, we found your time capsule in the attic!" Olivia said. She was dressed up in her grandmother's old clothes and she was Hula-Hooping like a champ.

"Mother, you wore that stuff?" Olivia's mom asked.

"Of course," said Grandma. "And I was pretty good with the hoop in my day too."

"Want to give it a try now, Grandma?" asked Olivia.

"I'd love to," Grandma replied.
Grandma took the Hula-Hoop from Olivia and then put it around her own waist.
"I've still got it. Hula! Hula! Hula!" Grandma chanted.

"I'm glad I found your time capsule, Grandma," said Olivia. "If I hadn't, I might have never known all this about you."

"It's good for families to learn new things about one another and then remember those things," Grandma explained. "Now that you helped me remember *me* as a little girl, I hope I'll always remember you as a little girl."

Olivia had an idea. "I know how to help you remember! I'll make my own time capsule."

"Great idea. So, what should we put in it?" Grandma asked.

Olivia went through her closet and pulled out one of her dresses.

"Hmm . . . this one," Olivia decided.

"Definitely," Grandma answered.

Next, Grandma and Olivia searched through the yard.
Grandma held up a bat. "How about this?"
Olivia shook her head.

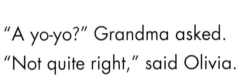

"A yo-yo?" Grandma asked.
"Not quite right," said Olivia.

"I've got it. Your jump rope?"
Grandma asked.
Olivia smiled. "Perfect."

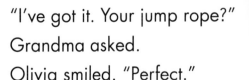

Olivia and Grandma spent the rest of the day looking around the house for other items that Olivia could put into her time capsule. They even found her favorite bow when they took a peek under the couch.

"Nice to see you kids playing together," Dad said.

Olivia chose a few more things to put in her trunk—even her special sunglasses!

"These are very excellent choices, Olivia," Grandma said as they looked at everything Olivia had added to the time capsule. "I think it's just about complete."

"I feel like it needs just one more thing," Olivia said as she looked around the attic.

"Well, let's see. The camera from my time capsule still has film in it," Grandma said.

"What's film?" asked Olivia.

"I'll show you," answered Grandma, and she held out the camera, clicked a button, and a piece of paper came out of it.

"One more," Grandma said and clicked the button again.

"These pictures will be ready in a jiffy. Two minutes tops."

Olivia was shocked. "You had to wait two whole minutes to see your pictures when you were a girl?"

As Olivia watched the paper, a picture of her and her grandmother appeared.

"This is what my time capsule was missing!" Olivia said.

"Mine too," replied Grandma.

They put a photo into each of their trunks, and then they hugged.

At nighttime, Grandma tucked Olivia
into bed.
"Thank you, Olivia," she said. "It was
fun to remember when I was your age."
"This day will be fun to remember too,"
Olivia said as Grandma gave her a kiss.
"Indeed, it will," Grandma said. "Good
night, Olivia."
"Good night, Grandma," Olivia said.